STAR

COLOR ZOO

Lois Ehlert

HarperCollinsPublishers

Dedicated to Jim, Jane, and Margaret

Color Zoo
Copyright © 1989 by Lois Ehlert
Manufactured in China. All rights reserved.
20 19 18 17 16

Typography by Bettina Rossner

Library of Congress Cataloging-in-Publication Data
Ehlert, Lois.
    Color zoo.

Summary: Introduces colors and shapes
with illustrations of shapes that form animal faces
when placed on top of one another.

1. Color—Study and teaching (Elementary)—Juvenile literature.
2. Visual perception—Study and teaching (Elementary)—Juvenile literature.
[1. Shape. 2. color] I. Title.

ND1490.E35 1989   701'.8   87-17065
ISBN 0-397-32259-3
ISBN 0-397-32260-7 (lib. bdg.)

Shapes and colors in your zoo,

Lots of things that you can do.

Heads and ears, beaks and snouts,

That's what animals are all about.

I know animals and you do too;

Make some new ones for your zoo.

TIGER

CIRCLE

FOX

TRIANGLE

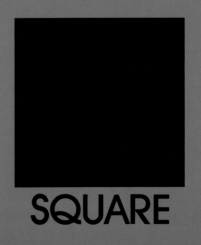

SQUARE

TRIANGLE

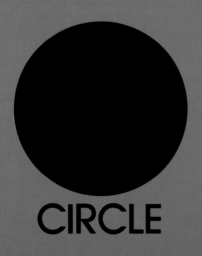

CIRCLE

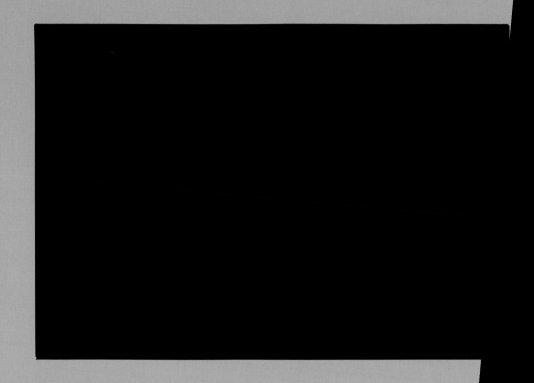

RECTANGLE

MOU USE

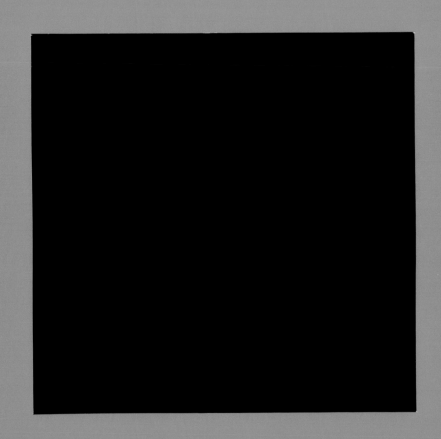

SQUARE

MONKEY

OVAL

DEER

HEART

RECTANGLE

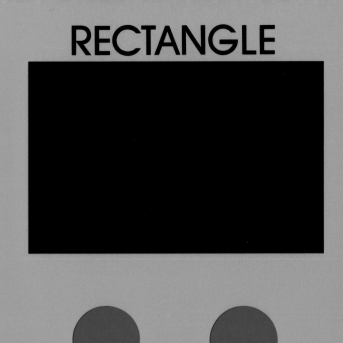

OVAL

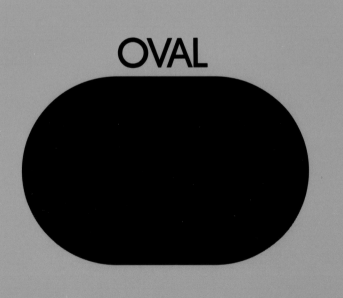

HEART

LION

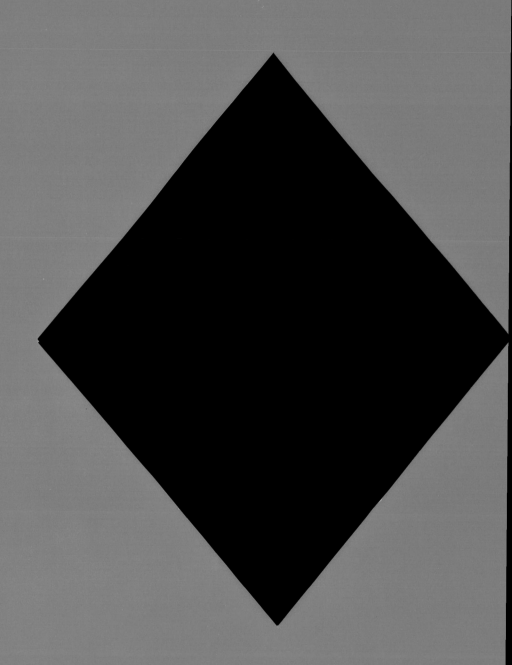

DIAMOND

GOAT

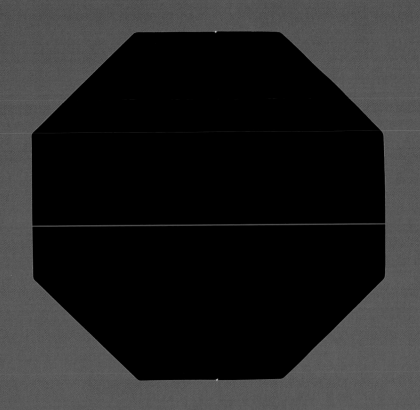

OCTAGON

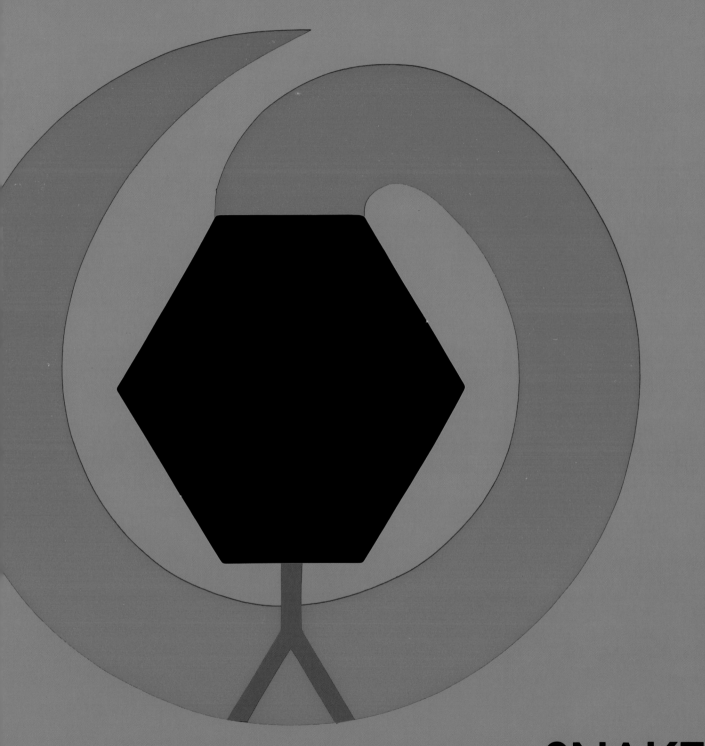

SNAKE

HEXAGON

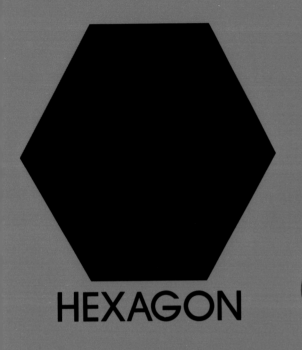

HEXAGON

OCTAGON

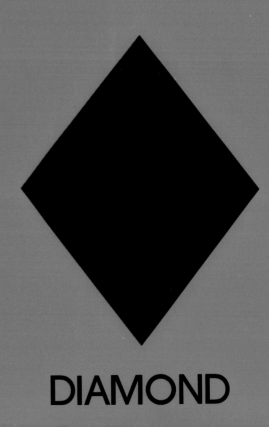

DIAMOND

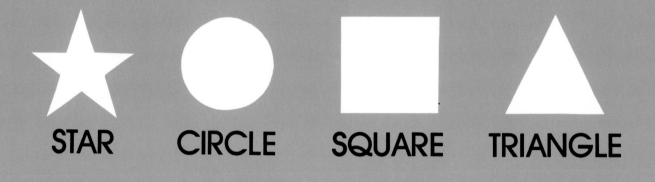

STAR   CIRCLE   SQUARE   TRIANGLE

RECTANGLE   HEART   OVAL

DIAMOND   OCTAGON   HEXAGON

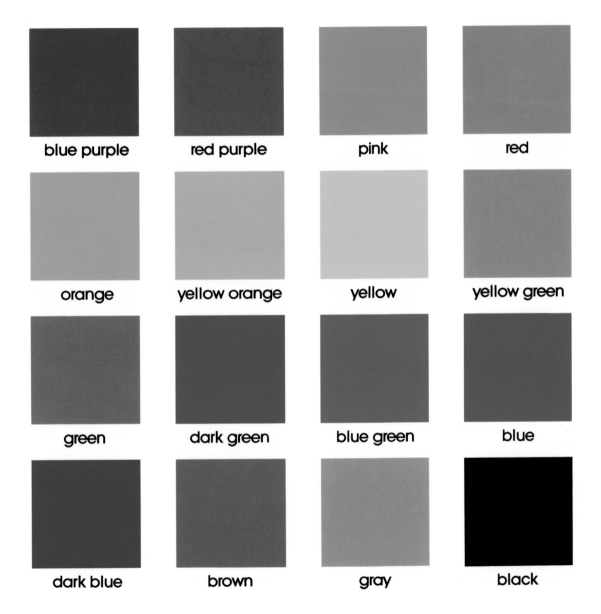

blue purple	red purple	pink	red
orange	yellow orange	yellow	yellow green
green	dark green	blue green	blue
dark blue	brown	gray	black

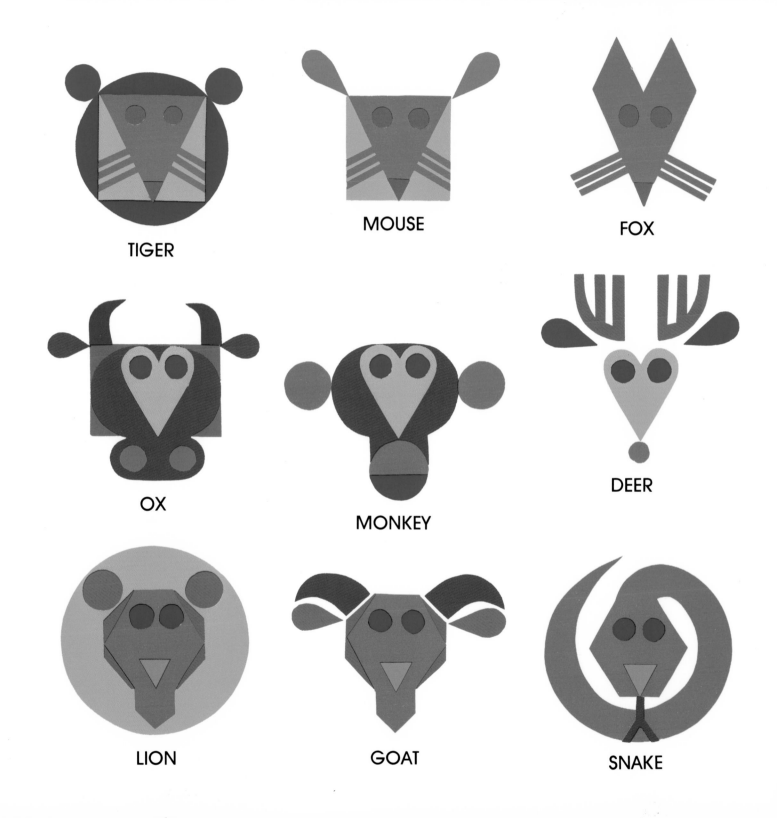

TIGER

MOUSE

FOX

OX

MONKEY

DEER

LION

GOAT

SNAKE